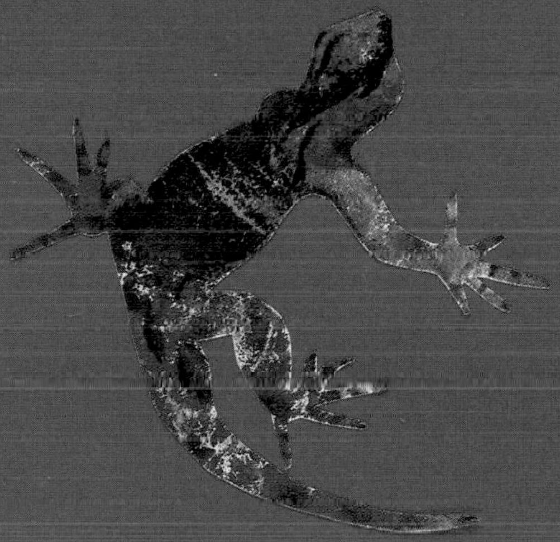

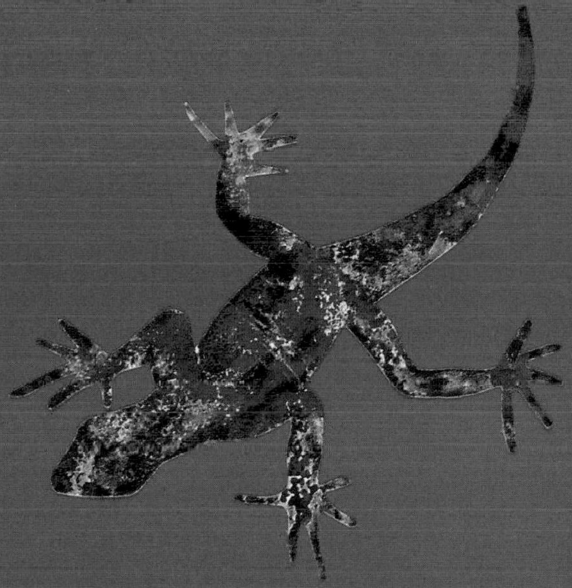

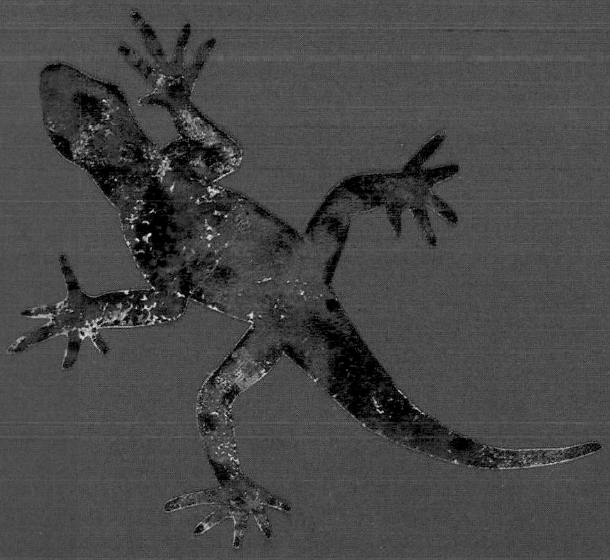

The House
That Jack Built

pictures by JENNY STOW

Dial Books for Young Readers

New York

First published in the United States 1992
by Dial Books for Young Readers
A Division of Penguin Books USA Inc.
375 Hudson Street · New York, New York 10014

Published in Great Britain by Frances Lincoln Limited
Pictures copyright © 1992 by Jenny Stow
All rights reserved
Printed in Hong Kong
First Edition
10 9 8 7 6 5 4 3 2 1

Library of Congress Cataloging in Publication Data
House that Jack built.
The house that Jack built / pictures by Jenny Stow.
p.   cm.
Summary: The familiar cumulative nursery rhyme is
illustrated with scenes placing the characters in a
Caribbean setting.
ISBN 0-8037-1090-9
1. Nursery rhymes. 2. Children's poetry.
[1. Nursery rhymes.]   I. Stow, Jenny, Ill. II. Title.
PZ8.3.H79 1992   398.8—dc20   91–23850   CIP   AC

The illustrations for this book are collages rendered
in paint, ink, and crayon. To create different textures,
color was added using various techniques that
include rubbing, rolling, and sponging.

For Jack

This is the house that Jack built.

This is the malt
That lay in the house that Jack built.

This is the rat,
That ate the malt
That lay in the house that Jack built.

This is the cat,
That killed the rat,
That ate the malt
That lay in the house that Jack built.

This is the dog,
That worried the cat,
That killed the rat,
That ate the malt
That lay in the house that Jack built.

This is the cow with the crumpled horn,
That tossed the dog,
That worried the cat,
That killed the rat,
That ate the malt
That lay in the house that Jack built.

This is the maiden all forlorn,
That milked the cow with the crumpled horn,
That tossed the dog,
That worried the cat,
That killed the rat,
That ate the malt
That lay in the house that Jack built.

This is the man all tattered and torn,
That kissed the maiden all forlorn,
That milked the cow with the crumpled horn,
That tossed the dog,
That worried the cat,
That killed the rat,
That ate the malt
That lay in the house that Jack built.

This is the priest all shaven and shorn,
That married the man all tattered and torn,
That kissed the maiden all forlorn,
That milked the cow with the crumpled horn,
That tossed the dog,
That worried the cat,
That killed the rat,
That ate the malt
That lay in the house that Jack built.

This is the cock that crowed in the morn,
That waked the priest all shaven and shorn,
That married the man all tattered and torn,
That kissed the maiden all forlorn,
That milked the cow with the crumpled horn,
That tossed the dog,
That worried the cat,
That killed the rat,
That ate the malt
That lay in the house that Jack built.

This is the farmer sowing his corn,
That kept the cock that crowed in the morn,
That waked the priest all shaven and shorn,
That married the man all tattered and torn,
That kissed the maiden all forlorn,
That milked the cow with the crumpled horn,
That tossed the dog,
That worried the cat,
That killed the rat,
That ate the malt
That lay in the house that Jack built.

This is the house that Jack built.

11
2.50

12-93